W9-DDA-719

Real Life Stories

RANCHING

Rennay Craats

— Weigl Publishers Inc. —

About *Ranching*

This book is based on the real life accounts of the people who settled the American West. History is brought to life through quotes from personal journals, letters to family back home, and historical records of those who traveled West to build a better life.

Published by Weigl Publishers Inc.
123 South Broad Street, Box 227
Mankato, MN 56002
USA

Web site: www.weigl.com
Copyright ©2003 WEIGL PUBLISHERS INC.

Library of Congress Cataloging-in-Publication Data

Craats, Rennay.
    Ranching / Rennay Craats.
        p. cm. -- (Real life stories series)
    Summary: Briefly explores what it was like to live and work on a ranch in the latter half of the nineteenth century, including first-hand accounts from people who owned, managed, or just lived on ranches.
    Includes bibliographical references and index.
    ISBN 1-59036-081-8 (library bound : alk. paper)
    1. Ranch life--West (U.S.)--Juvenile literature. 2. Ranch life
  --West (U.S.)--History--Juvenile literature. 3. West (U.S.)--History--Juvenile literature. 4. West (U.S.)-
  -Social life and customs--Juvenile literature.   [1. Ranch life--West (U.S.)--History.   2. West (U.S.)--
History. 3. West (U.S.)--Social life and customs.]   I. Title. II. Series.
    F596.C885 2003
    636'.01'097809034--dc21

                                        2002012726

Printed in the United States of America
1 2 3 4 5 6 7 8 9 0   06 05 04 03 02

Photograph Credits
Cover: Denver Public Library, Western History Department (Z-653); **Colorado Historical Society:** page 14 (CHS.X6134); **Corbis Corporation:** page 21R; **Denver Public Library Western History Department:** pages 1 (X-21563), 3 (Z-653), 4 (K-45), 6 (Z-653), 8 (MCC-1848), 16 (Z-1248), 18 (BS-47); **Glenbow Archives:** pages 10 (NA-2556-5), 22 (NC-39-289); **Photo Courtesy of the South Dakota State Historical Society-State Archives:** page 12/13; **Wyoming State Archives:** page 21L (Kirkland #9).

Text Credits
Excerpt on page 11: Ingalls Wilder, Laura. *On the Banks of Plum Creek*. New York: HarperCollins Juvenile Books, 1953.

Project Coordinator	Copy Editor	Layout
Michael Lowry	Frances Purslow	Terry Paulhus
Substantive Editor	**Design**	**Photo Research**
Christa Bedry	Virginia Boulay & Bryan Pezzi	Dylan Kirk & Daorcey Le Bray

Contents

Big Business

Life on a ranch was exciting. Ranch workers roped and herded cattle. They also tamed horses. Ranchers created symbols for their ranches to keep track of all their cattle. The cattle on a ranch were **branded** with this symbol. A brand showed everyone which animals belonged to which rancher.

Cities and towns began to grow quickly in the mid-1800s. Ranchers raised **livestock** to help feed the townspeople. The ranching industry grew. Many small ranches became big businesses. More than 10 million cattle were sold between 1865 and 1885. Tens of thousands of cowboys were hired on ranches. Cowboys fixed fences and cleaned the stables. They also fed the cows and fixed the buildings. Cowboys guarded the bosses' cattle.

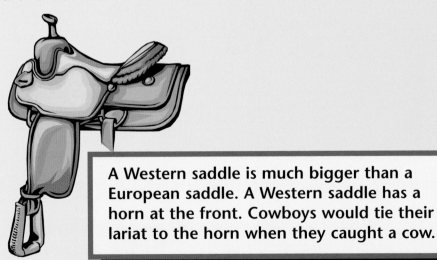

A Western saddle is much bigger than a European saddle. A Western saddle has a horn at the front. Cowboys would tie their lariat to the horn when they caught a cow.

The Lasso

Cowboys used lariats or lassos to catch cows. The word lariat comes from the Spanish words *la reata*, which mean "tie up."

Building a Ranch

Some ranch owners were called **cattle barons**. They were businesspeople. Many cattle barons had never lived or worked on a ranch. They owned thousands of cattle and huge pieces of land. The daily running of the ranch was left to ranch managers and trusted cowboys. Some ranch owners were once young ranch hands. They worked their way up to owning their own land.

Cowboys often wore chaps to protect their legs from thorns and branches along the trails. Some chaps were made of sheepskin to keep their legs warm.

Real Life Stories

"Under Mr. Bailey's efficient management, the property progressed at an almost unbelievable pace. The herds of cattle ... reached about 60,000 head; the horses ... were counted in the many hundreds ... This progress was all accomplished by Mr. Bailey before 1900."

James B. Barker

Cattle Thieves

Ranchers had to guard against people trying to steal their cattle. Some cattle thieves stole livestock in the night. Others stole cattle in broad daylight. Ranchers hired cowboys to **drive** their cattle to the railroad stations. Some of the cowboys sold the cattle and kept the money for themselves. Ranchers began sending permanent employees on the drives to protect their cattle.

The Spanish were the first ranchers. They were called *vaqueros*. This is Spanish for "those who work with cows." In the United States, the word was changed to "buckaroos."

Real Life Stories

"This was about 1871 or 1872 and everyone was driving cattle to Abilene, Kansas, the end of the railroad, where they could sell their fat cattle. My father let a firm … have his cattle and they never brought him back a cent. The Olive family lived just north of us and were good friends of ours, and good reliable men, who would have taken our cattle and brought back the money, but my father picked the wrong men."

James C. Shaw

A Natural Enemy

Ranchers and farmers relied on nature. Bad weather or a **plague** of insects could destroy crops. Crops were needed to feed people and livestock. Horses became too weak to work or be ridden to town without feed. Sometimes livestock and horses starved.

Some tornadoes were strong enough to rip the walls and roofs off buildings.

Real Life Stories

"A cloud was over the sun. It was not like a cloud they had ever seen before. It was a cloud of something like snowflakes, but they were larger than snowflakes, and thin and glittering … The cloud was grasshoppers. Their bodies hid the sun and made darkness. Their thin, large wings gleamed and glittered. The rasping whirring of their wings filled the whole air and they hit the ground and the house with the noise of a hailstorm."

Laura Ingalls Wilder

Life on the Ranch

Large ranches were made up of several buildings. Some buildings were the homes of the workers or the rancher. Other buildings held equipment or animals.

The cowboys trained the horses in a corral. The corral was close to the stables.

The horses were kept in a building called a stable.

The cowboys lived in a building called the bunkhouse. The bunkhouse was one large room filled with beds, tables, and chairs.

The ranch house was the largest and fanciest building on the ranch. The rancher and his family lived in the ranch house.

Every cowboy knew where the mess hall was. It was the small building near the bunkhouse. The cooks served dinner in the mess hall.

Far From Anywhere

Ranches were often many days' travel away from the markets. Ranchers did not want to forget items on their lists. They would have to live without the forgotten items until the next trip into town. Everything else that ranchers needed was made or grown on the ranch.

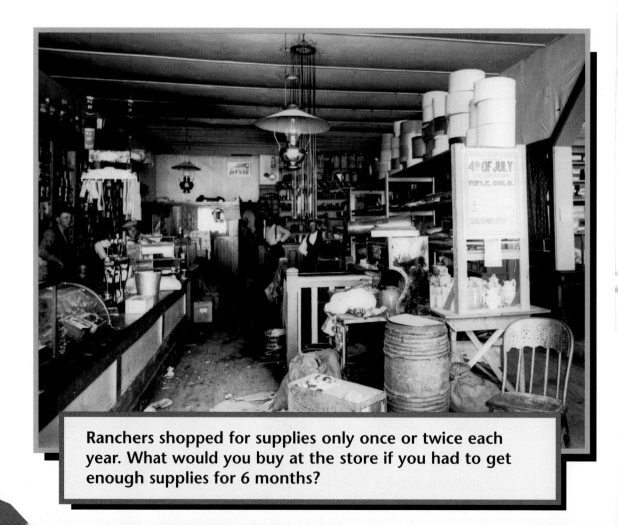

Ranchers shopped for supplies only once or twice each year. What would you buy at the store if you had to get enough supplies for 6 months?

Real Life Stories

"You bought beans … 500 pounds a year in 100-pound sacks. Each rancher had sort of a little **commissary***, a room outside that he kept locked, where he kept supplies. They only [went to the market] maybe twice a year. It was done by wagon, and … you camped out on your way … I remember that as being most fun. The camping out was marvelous."*

Thelma Rawls Fletcher

Growing Gardens

Ranchers raised livestock. That was how they made money. Still, there was more to ranching than cattle and sheep. Early ranchers farmed as well. Nearly all ranchers kept a large garden plot. This garden grew fruits and vegetables for food.

Ranchers and cowboys had large gardens that grew fresh fruits and vegetables.

Real Life Stories

*"Every rancher had a garden … they
didn't have fresh vegetables if they
didn't have a garden because you didn't
have neighbors. Your neighbor was
usually 15 or 20 miles away. And,
so every rancher had a garden and
an* **orchard** *… And then the women …
did the canning and dried the fruit."*

Thelma Rawls Fletcher

The Railroad

Ranches were spread out across the United States. Some ranches stood along the route to the cattle markets. Ranching changed when the east–west railroad was finished in 1869. Goods could reach the other side of the country in less than 2 weeks by train. It had taken more than 4 months to transport goods by wagon. The railroad opened up new possibilities for ranchers in western states, such as California, Colorado, Montana, Texas, and Wyoming. These ranchers could now sell cattle to Americans all along the railway lines.

After the railroad was built, cowboys did not have to drive their cattle as far as they once did.

Major Railroads
in the 1880s

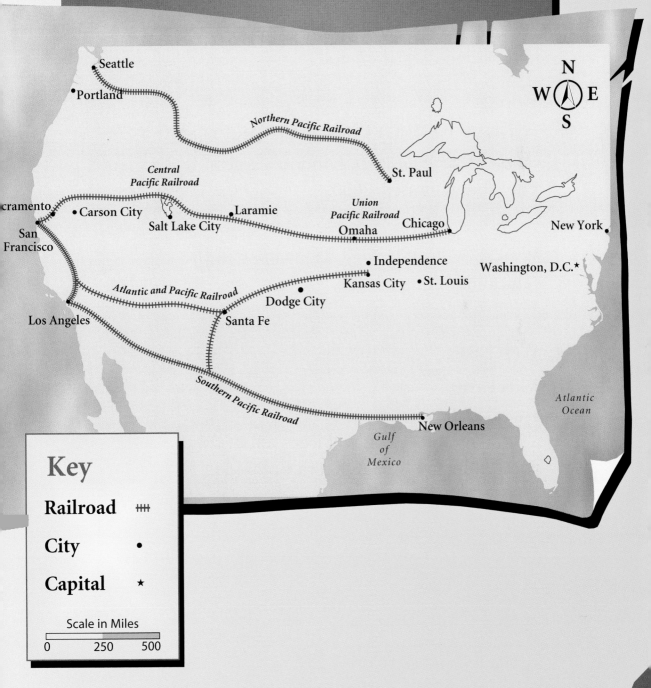

Key

Railroad ┼┼┼

City •

Capital ★

Scale in Miles

0   250   500

Learning More about Ranching

To learn more about ranching, you can borrow books from the library or surf the Internet.

Books

Harrison, Peter and Norman Bancroft Hunt. *World of the Wild West*. London: Anness Publishing Limited, 2000.

Wrobel, Scott. *Ranching*. Mankato: Creative Education, 1999.

Web Sites

Kids Farm
www.kidsfarm.com
Visitors to Kids Farm will learn about the animals and people that live on a ranch in Colorado.

Encarta
www.encarta.com
Enter the search word "ranching" into an online encyclopedia, such as Encarta.

Compare and Contrast

Life on the ranch is similar now to what it was for early ranchers in many ways. Some things have changed. Look at the photographs below. Compare the present-day ranch with the one from the 1800s. How is the modern ranch on the right the same as the early ranch on the left? How are they different?

What Have You Learned?

Based on what you have just read, try to answer the following questions.

2

True or false? Ranchers could always trust their cowboys.

1

Who were the cattle barons?

a) cattle thieves
b) ranch owners
c) Spanish ranchers
d) cowboys

3

When was the east–west railroad completed?

a) 1823
b) 1849
c) 1856
d) 1869

4

True or false? The bunkhouse was where the cowboys lived on a ranch.

5

What was the mess hall?

a) a cowboy's bedroom
b) a stable for horses
c) where the cowboys ate
d) an outhouse

6

True or false? Ranchers had to buy all of their food from farmers.

Answers

1. b
2. False. Some cowboys stole money and cattle from the ranchers.
3. d
4. True
5. c
6. False. Ranchers grew their own fruit and vegetables.

Words to Know

branded: marked on the hide to be identified

cattle barons: rich ranchers who were also businessmen

commissary: a place where food and equipment were sold or kept

drive: move cattle to a new pasture or to the market

livestock: cattle or horses

orchard: a piece of land that grows fruit or nut trees

plague: a sudden outbreak that causes great damage

Index